Cuckoo
can't find
You

Lorianne Siomades

SCHOLASTIC INC.
New York Toronto London Auckland Sydney
Mexico City New Delhi Hong Kong Buenos Aires

For
Madison

Can you help Cuckoo
and his friends
find the things
they are looking for?

Bear can't find his pear.

Crow can't find her bow.

Fox can't find her socks.

Stork can't find his fork.

Snail can't find her pail.

Goat can't find her boat.

Fish can't find her dish.

Seal can't find his wheel.

Bat can't find his hat.

Loon can't find her spoon.

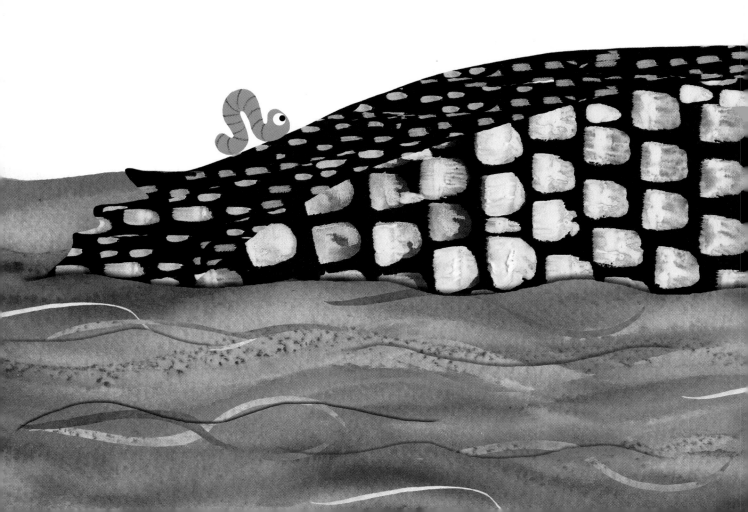

Bug can't find her mug.

Ram can't find his jam.

Bee can't find his key.

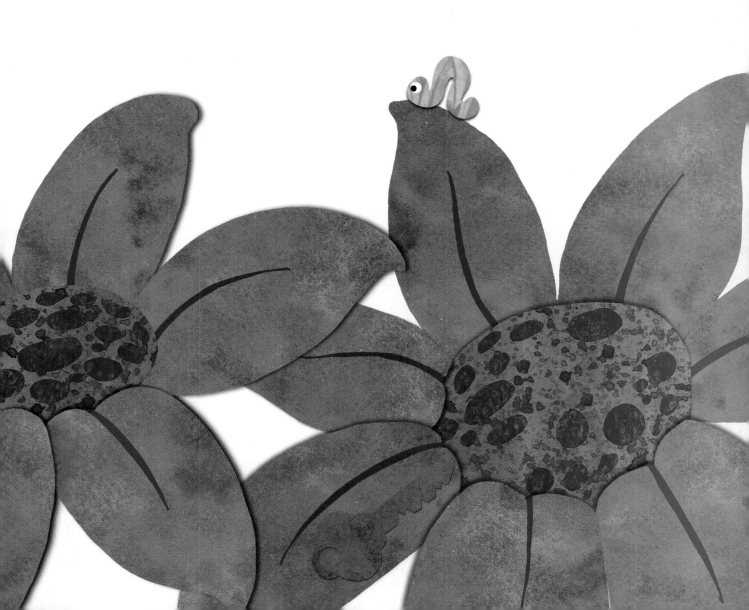

Cuckoo can't find you.

Place your child's photo here.

ISBN 0-439-56618-5

Copyright © 2002 by Lorianne Siomades. All rights reserved. Published by Scholastic Inc.,
557 Broadway, New York, NY 10012, by arrangement with Boyds Mills Press.
SCHOLASTIC and associated logos are trademarks and/or registered trademarks of Scholastic Inc.

12 11 10 9 8 7 6 5 4 3 2 1   3 4 5 6 7 8/0

Printed in the U.S.A.   23

First Scholastic printing, October 2003

The text of this book is set in 24-point Times Bold.